ANA & HER BOSS

Damien Dsoul

ANA & HER BOSS

4PLAY PRESS

Prologue

The logs of wood kindled with flame in the fireplace. Soaring Bach filtered the speakers and enveloped the room. Alek, and his wife Ana, lay on the divan in their night clothes, kissing. Alek roamed his hand over his wife's breasts from under her nightgown, tweaking her erect nipples, then slid his fingers downward to massage the tiny forest of her pubic region. She raised one leg over his thigh to give him suitable access.

"So," he muttered softly while he nuzzled her ear.

"So?" she replied.

"Aren't you going to tell me about it?"

She giggled. "I don't know if I should."

"Come on, you know you will. I'm dying to hear what happened."

"Nothing happened, darling. He took me to his suite and we fucked. That's all."

"I know that, my darling, slutty munch-kin. But I want to know everything. How it all started with both of you." He nibbled on her earlobe. This elicited further excitement from his wife.

"But darling, I've already told you everything that's happened between us. You know just about everything."

"Not everything," he insisted. "I don't know what happened this evening before you got home. I'd like to hear everything from the beginning, if you don't mind."

"I'm afraid you might get jealous."

"That's silly. I've never gotten jealous before."

"No, you haven't. But there's always a first time."

"This isn't our first time doing such. I've never been angry before, why would I be now."

She gave him a serious look. "Do you promise?"

"I promise. I love you too much to think of that."

She drew in her breath sharply as he slipped his middle finger into her pussy. He flicked his thumb against the jutting knob that was her clit. Her juices poured down his finger and a second later he added another finger into her snatch and went on finger-fucking her slowly. She had been well fucked earlier on by her black boss, before she returned home from work nearly an hour ago. Although Alex hadn't yet seen the two of them in action, he was aware of much of the details; that her black boss had a thick cock, and according to his wife, he *really* knew how to work it. Ana had confessed all her sex adventures to him. Alek gushed with anticipation at seeing the two of them together screwing.

Ana grasped his tent-pole erection inside his shorts and gave it a gentle squeeze.

"You're being a naughty boy, darling," she said to him. "I'll tell you everything as it's what you want to hear. But first, would you mind refilling my champagne?" She showed him her empty wine glass.

Alek turned to his left and grabbed the neck of a *Dom Perignon* champagne bottle out of the ice bucket, and filled her glass as well as his.

"To a happy marriage and a lovely anniversary

with you, honey," he said to her before they clinked their glasses.

"And to you, my love," she said. "Happy anniversary."

They took a sip of the wine and smacked their lips from its exquisite taste. Alek tastes the wine between her rosy lips and tongue; their fluids exchanged as their tongues flicked against each other.

"Now," he dropped his glass on the table next to the wine bucket. "You were going to tell me a story?"

"Indeed I was." She got up from the divan and knelt before him, sensuously rubbing her hands on his thighs. "But I still don't know if I should."

"Awww, come on, darling, stop being a tease. You know how I hate it when you keep me in suspense like this."

"Yes, I do. Alright then, I'll tell. But first, you're going to have to lie back. You'll enjoy the story if you're relaxed."

Her hands pulled his shorts down his legs, freeing his cock from its temporary prison. Ana admired the sight of her husband's cock as it waved before her face. She wrapped both hands around it and stroked softly. Her tongue slid over her lips; she looked like someone about to devour a favourite delicacy. Her hand drew the foreskin of his cock up and down, stroked a stream of pre-cum out the tiny aperture of his cock. Alek felt like a wounded animal before her. She knew just how to take control over him when she wanted to, and most times he loved it when she displayed her dominant side to him when they made love.

7

"Do you want to hear the story of how my boss and I first got noticed?" she asked the question with a salacious look in her eyes. "You're going to promise to be a good boy while I tell it, won't you?"

"Yes, yes, I promise," Alex gasped at what she was doing to him.

"I can't hear you, darling." She gave the head of his cock a slap. "Say it loud, darling; that you're going to be a good boy while you listen."

"Yes!" he said louder. "Yes, I promise to be a good boy."

Ana softened at this. "Good," she murmured. She gave the head of his cock a kiss. Alek felt like melting when she did it. "It started a week ago …"

Chapter 1 - One Week Ago

Ana drove her Volkswagen 'Bug' into the parking space situated by the right side of the two-storey, glass-fronted foreign agency building where she worked. She got out of her car and bent to push several locks of her short-cropped blonde hair from her face. She wore maroon lipstick which matched her maroon jacket and knee-length skirt she was wearing. Her feet were enclosed in a pair of ankle-length boots. Finished preening herself, she slung her handbag over her shoulder and walked around the back of her car towards the building's front. Little did she know, a pair of eyes had watched her perform her little check-up when she'd gotten out of her vehicle.

Ana had been working with the agency for three years now, and not once had she received a black mark against her, regarding her work ethics. She was always punctual, cordial and friendly with everybody in her office and was someone people went to if they needed someone to hear out their troubles. Her boss was well aware of her traits, which was why he'd taken the time to arrive at work a half hour before she did. He always got a kick out of watching her alight from her vehicle, checking out whatever outfit she had on and noting how exacting delectable they looked on her.

Ana was a beautiful woman. Almost all her male colleagues knew this, and they seldom ceased making 'off' comments about her. One person who took it seriously was her boss, Dennis Hammond, a

Black-American in his mid-fifties.

Every time he stood by his window ogling as she arrived at work, every time he walked past her office as she sat at her desk, thoughts of what lay underneath those clothes were all that ran through his mind. The fact that she was married did little to deter these thoughts from his head. Always, whenever he stopped by her to compliment her, his eyes ran all over her body, practically undressing her. He imagined what sort of bra and panties she would be wearing if she wore any, at all. Since arriving here in Zagreb four months ago, he'd distinctly sampled as much of the city that he could find time to indulge himself on: architecture, history, cuisine, and most especially the women, which often involved getting in sync with the city's night life.

Truth be told, Dennis was a man of wily charm, and nothing gave him greater joy than breaking women who often proved difficult for him. He could have his pick from the number of pretty lasses working in the agency, under his supervision... but none of them stood, compared to Ana. Her slender frame, short-cropped hair, light-brown eyes and lovely nose, topped off with a thin pair of lips... lips that sure could do well enough when put to work, Dennis smiled to himself.

He looked at his watch, then returned to his chair and pretended to be busy. In a few minutes he knew, his targeted lass was going to knock on his door as she almost always did, every morning. It was a ritual of hers and he'd instigated that she kept up with it.

Like clockwork, just one minute later, there

was a knock on his door before it came open, and in came Ana. She smiled at him as she approached his desk. He looked up from some papers in his hand and gave her his usual looking-over with a smile on his lips.

"Good morning, Mr. Hammond." She stopped in front of his desk.

"Good morning, Ana." Dennis got up from his chair, roaming his eyes about her. "You're looking as fine and lovely as a rose petal this morning."

Ana laughed shyly. Her boss never ceased flattering her; she couldn't help enjoying his remarks. A part of her enjoyed flirting with him just as much. He might be old, but he had a lot of fire still in him, and he always looked tough and handsome in his well-cut suits like the one he had on right now.

"Why, thank you, Mr. Hammond."

"Ana, you're hurting me deeply." He approached her from around his desk and came to a halt in front of her. "I've told you time after time, call me Dennis. Only the new faces in this agency call me 'sir', or 'Mr. Hammond', and you're not one of them."

She apologised. "I'm sorry, Dennis. I'm just too used to it."

"Well, it's time you get un-used to it. You're looking very beautiful today." His eyes sized her up from the crown of her hair down to the toes of her boots. "M-hmmm, you're husband's really taking good care of you."

"He tries his best, Dennis," she answered. "Well, Sir, I'd better head down to my desk."

She turned and left his office with the feeling

that his eyes were glued to her behind. Ana loved the attention and instinctively uplifted her ass any time he was around, knowing he was watching. Dennis felt an awakening in his pants and in his mind he imagined all that he'd love to do to that lovely body of hers.

Ana left his office and went down the stairs to where her cubicle desk was at. She unbuttoned her jacket, exchanging greetings with several of her colleagues before settling down to the day's work.

***

Ana was busy typing out a memo in her desktop computer when her boss's face loomed over her cubicle. Music was pouring off her computer's speakers and she was lost in them and barely noticed Dennis standing close to her until she looked up, startled to find him standing there.

He dropped a file folder on her desk. "This was excellent work you did, Ana. How come you're still here?" he glanced at his wristwatch. "It's almost noon: Time for lunch."

Ana turned down the volume of her music. "Sorry sir, but I don't have enough time for lunch. I asked Erika earlier to get me a Coke when she gets back."

"Just a Coke?" he asked with dismay. "Nonsense. Come with me, I know a good restaurant."

"But sir, I have these memos—"

"I'll get Jaro to handle it. Right now, you're going to have lunch with me. Meet me downstairs in five." He turned around and left.

His voice was bold and authoritative, and Ana couldn't help being moved by it. She turned off her

12

system and picked up her handbag, put on her shoes and left her cubicle.

He was waiting for her in the lobby. He hooked her arm in his and together they stepped out of the revolving glass doors into the hot afternoon sun. He directed her towards his custom Mercedes C-Class and she slid herself into the passenger seat. Her skirt momentarily rode up her thighs and Dennis got an eyeful of her pristine flesh before she made herself comfortable beside him. He turned the engine and drove out of the parking lot into the city.

He drove to the Restaurant 'Vinodol', where he usually had a reserved table. Ana knew about the restaurant, though had never thought of having lunch there before; their meals were too expensive for her. The head waiter led them to their table and took their order before leaving them.

"Ever been here before?" Dennis asked Ana.

"Not once, no," she answered. "It looks lovely inside."

"That's because you're here," he said. "You don't know how beautiful you are right now."

Ana couldn't help blushing. "You flatter me too much, Dennis."

"Call it what you may, but it's the truth. You're far too beautiful, and if I were your husband, I'd be over-jealous every time I let you leave home."

Their meals arrived minutes later and they dug into it. Dennis ordered a bottle of white wine and the hour ran along while they kept eating. Done with their meal, sipping the fine wine, Dennis made his move.

"Err... Ana, I heard some of the other girls in the office gossiping the other day that you're soon to celebrate your wedding anniversary. Is that true?"

Ana hesitated for a moment before answering. In her mind she wondered how he would have come across that information. Surely she hadn't gone around telling everyone in the office, most of whom she knew tattled a lot. "Yes, my husband and IW have been married five years now."

"Ah, congratulations to you both. I have a present for you but I forgot to bring it to the office. I was wondering if you wouldn't mind accompanying me to my home so I can give it to you."

"Sir, would that be necessary?"

"Oh yes, very necessary," he muttered. "You see, it's a very special gift. One I doubt your man's ever thought of giving you. It would be a great honour to me if you would accept it. I know you'll really like it."

His voice was as smooth as ice. He brought his hand over hers and he traced a line softly on her skin while he held her with his voice and eyes which seemed to burn straight into hers. He was unlike any man Ana had ever met. How strong and confident he felt in himself, everything about him oozed masculinity. What was ironic, was that she was starting to feel herself drawn to him. There was a weird, exciting sensation taking place right between her legs and she thought she could feel her nipples perking from inside her bra. It had been a while since she felt this sudden type of excitement come onto her, and right now she was at a loss as to how to handle it.

"Excuse me, Dennis," she got up from her chair. "I'd like to go powder my nose a little."

She left him and went in the direction of the

14

women's room.

Some minutes later she returned, smiling, and asked if they could leave now so he could fetch her the present he'd talked about. Dennis settled the bill quickly and once again hooked her arm around his and led her outside.

Chapter 2

Dennis lived in a posh apartment block not too far from the heart of the city. He parked outside and they entered the building and took an elevator to the fourth floor where he resided. He couldn't help touching Ana on the way up, holding her hand in his as they got to his door. With his free hand he fished out his key, unlocked the door and ushered her inside.

Everything about his apartment was ultramodern: the LCD home theatre, the stereo beside it, the interior décor and thick white carpet that lay in the centre of the living room. Dennis told her to make herself comfortable as he unbuttoned his suit jacket and draped it over the back of a couch. He went in the direction of a corridor leading further into his apartment. Ana dropped her handbag and sat down, but he wasn't gone for long. Dennis had taken off his shirt as well, and returned wearing just his vest and pants, carrying an exotic shopping bag in his hand.

"Happy Anniversary," he said as he gave it to her. I think there should be a sentence or two in here about her reaction to seeing him without his shirt on – her surprise or her reaction to his body?

"Thank you, Dennis." She accepted the bag and took out the black square-shaped case that was inside. Her features bore signs that she was curious about whatever could be inside.

"Open it," he demanded.

She did so, and nothing quite prepared her for what she unearthed. It was a black spider-web lace,

16

long-sleeved shirt with matching panties and silk stockings. Ana held it before her face, felt her hand over its smooth, soft fabric. Her mouth hung open with joy and surprise she could barely utter any tangible word.

"Do you like it?" Dennis asked her.

"My God. It's beautiful!" She broke into surprised laughter. "Really, Dennis, I can't begin to thank you for this."

"How about you try it out for me." He sat down on the couch across from her. "You can go into my room and change if you like."

Ana looked at him, shocked by his suggestion. "Are you serious?"

"I am indeed. I need to know how well it fits you. I told the shop I'd get back to them in twenty-four hours if it doesn't match. Go on, I'll wait for you, here."

Seeing no harm in it, Ana took everything with her towards the direction of his bedroom he'd pointed it out to her. She closed the door and started taking off her clothes.

Dennis was listening to a reggae jam from his CD collection when Ana returned from the bedroom. She called out to him, and he turned around and this time it was his turn to drop his jaw. Ana looked transformed with the lingerie outfit she now had on. Along with the panties and stockings, she looked like a white wife about to become a hungry slut. Her cheeks glowed red as she smiled and pirouetted on her feet. I think you can make this paragraph sound sexier by going into a little more detail about how the fabric clings or flows from her skin or perhaps how her body curves in the right places, etc...

"Well, what do you think?" She asked him.

Dennis got up and approached her. Ana saw the pressing bulge in his pants and Dennis smiled, wanting her to notice it. She gulped down air as she pictured the thick black snake that must be itching to jump out of his pants right then and there. Suddenly her horniness kicked into overdrive. Her pussy gave her an itch—it needed to be scratched.

He came to her and grabbed her by the arm and propelled her roughly towards him. Ana nearly fell on him. His large hands grasped her butt and gave her ass cheeks a tight squeeze while he jammed his tongue down her throat. Ana grunted, at the same time subsiding herself to his lecherous kiss. He pulled up her legs and she, knowing what he wanted, jumped upon him while he held her up. She wrapped her thin legs around his waistline and kissed him back hungrily. Dennis held her ass with one hand and unzipped his fly with the other, and out sprung his 10" cock. Her arms wrapped around his neck, balancing herself while he tucked her panties to the side and the bulbous head of his cock found the entrance to her cunt. Ana held her breath and barked a cry as his cock gained entrance inside her and inch by inch slipped inside her pussy.

Ana cried out as inch after inch of his cock slid into her and her pussy walls spurt her juices all over it. Dennis held her up, pumping his cock further in and out of her. She held onto him for dear life and screamed as an orgasm exploded within her.

He fucked her like that for a while, grunting as he moved, before then lowering her on a sofa. Her legs rested on his shoulders and Dennis got into position and thrust his cock deeper inside her fuck hole. Ana grasped his shoulders and her moans rose like wildfire as he fucked her hard. She looked at the sight of his cock slipping in and out of her cunt, his shaft lathered with her pussy juice.

Dennis gasped from the way her pussy muscles constricted his shaft as if fighting for him to cum immediately; how he loved that feeling.

"Yeahhhh, that's some good pussy," he murmured. "That's some good fucking Croatian pussy right there!"

Ana was panting as if on fire. "Ohh… Oh God, I'm cumming! I'm cumminggggg!" she nearly fainted as another orgasmic burst went off inside her.

Dennis too, felt a growing tightness in his prick and knew that he was only moments away. He gritted his teeth and just at the last minute withdrew his pussy-stained shaft from within her and sprayed it over her pubic region. Both of them sighed with relief at this. His cock became flaccid almost instantly as he sat down beside her.

"I guess the outfit is a sure fit," he muttered, then laughed.

Ana joined him in laughing too.

Chapter 3

Alek was at home, anxiously waiting for his wife to return from work. It was approaching six in the evening; usually she got home before he did, around five-thirty or thereabouts. The agency where she worked was quite farther from their home, and as she usually took the car, it cut the distance by half.

He looked in the fridge, took out a beer, inserted a jazz CD in the stereo system and sat back and guzzled his beer and continued to wait. He tapped his hand on the chair's armrest, though not in time to the music he was listening to. He drummed his feet on the floor and glanced at his watch almost every minute, hoping the next would signal his Ana arriving home.

Impatiently, he drained his beer and switched off the stereo system, then went into the little room jutting off the side of the living room which served as his library. His desktop computer sat on a table and having nothing better to do, he booted his system and clicked on one of several home-made porn movies that featured him and Ana. It helped ease the nerves of his mind while he waited.

There were three self-recorded videos of them making love in their bedroom and living room, and one which had Ana making love to a man they'd met in Turkey last summer while vacationing there. It was this video he enjoyed watching and his hand pressed down on his erection inside his pants. He was lost in the video when there came the sound of a door coming open and then closing back. Alex shut down the video immediately and jumped out of his chair as if he'd been goosed. He stuck his head out the door and there was his lovely Ana. She dropped her handbag on the sofa then came to him, wrapped her arms around his waistline and kissed his lips.

"Hiya, darling," she said.

"You're late," he said.

"I'm sorry. I had lots of paperwork to cover at the agency." She walked past him towards the bedroom. Alex followed.

"That's not all that's kept you late today," he said, petulantly.

"Aw, darling, you don't trust me anymore?" she enquired over her shoulder as she stepped into the bedroom and began taking off her jacket.

"It's not that. But I want to know all of what happened between you and him."

"*All* of what happened, darling? And who's the 'he' in this?" she looked at him innocently.

"You know who. Don't tease me, Ana."

She gave a coquettish laugh, sitting on the bed and crossing one leg over the other. Alex could bet that she wasn't wearing any panties; the thought of it made his blood boil and his cock nudge its head inside his pants.

"Let's say I don't know whom you're talking about, darling." She flicked her tongue lasciviously at him and smiled. "Exactly what are you going to do about it?"

"I'm going to do this!" He dove at her. Ana might have been expecting something like this but she was taken aback by the speed at which he came at her.

She uttered a squeal of surprise, mixed with bursts of laughter as he pushed her on the bed and began working her skirt up her thighs. He grunted affirmatively when he found that she didn't have any panties on. He also noticed the pink swelling of her pussy lips, indicating that she'd just been well fucked. He slipped a finger inside her pussy and she gasped as he rolled his finger inside her, noticing how slippery she was.

"I knew it! I just knew you wouldn't have anything on. You fucked him didn't you?" he threw the question at her accusingly.

"And what if I did," she glowered at him playfully. "You knew I was going to fuck him. Why else would I call you at the restaurant's ladies' room, but to tell you about it?"

"Did you let him cum inside you?" He asked anxiously, still fingering her.

"No. I almost wanted him to, but thought it too early. But darling, he's got a lovely cock." She enunciated each word. "Thick, black and ravishing to look at."

Alex came off the bed and knelt before her with her legs spread before him. He had a yearning look on his face. His cock was struggling to be free from his pants. "Was he thicker than me?"

"I can't say, darling," she teased. "Although he's formidable, even a match to you. Matter of fact, I'd say he fucks better than you!"

That did it for Alek. He dove his head between his wife's legs, and she yelped with delight as his lips bit down on her pussy. She loved teasing him like this and he, too, enjoyed it. Often he was like a puppy reaching for a bone with her pulling back on

22

the leash. Whenever he left her to her own devices, he went practically crazy with excitement, wondering what she was up to, whom she was with—if she was even with a man—and what she could be doing with him. It is their lifestyle, and it always empowers them to cherish the love they have for one another.

Ana moaned softly. Her fingers undid the buttons of her blouse and pinched her bra-less nipples. She hiked her skirt up to her waist and rested her legs on his shoulders. Alex munched on her pussy like he was gobbling up ice cream, her juice lathering his lips. He slid his palms under his wife's ass and held her hips up to his face and went on sucking and lapping her cum. Ana's sighs alternated between highs and searing octave.

"Babe, you lick my pussy so good!" she cried out. "Nobody eats my pussy better than you!"

Her husband paused in his actions and said, "I'll bet they can't," then resumed eating up her pussy. He swirled and rotated his tongue around her pink orifice, then flicked the tip on his tongue under her clit. This sent shock waves crashing into Ana. She beat her head side to side of the bed, gasping as she felt the onrush of the inevitable. Alex too sensed she was close to cumming and increased his actions. He inserted two fingers into her pussy and finger-fucked her with maddening frenzy. Ana's breath caught in her throat in scattered bursts and she threw her head back as her body shook with convulsion and she released a shriek that was bound to give their neighbours boners. Alek never let go from sucking in the sweet, gushing nectar of her pussy as his wife had herself a heart-splitting

23

orgasm.

Only when finally her cries dissipated, did he then pull himself away from her. He lay on the bed beside her, listening to her gasping breaths. He swept her blonde hair off from her face. She looked so beautiful as she lay there beside him.

Her eyes inched open and smiled at him. Her hand went to her pussy and she slipped two fingers inside then brought them to her lips and sucked on them.

"Hmmmmm… so delicious," she moaned.

Alex bent his head and sucked on her right breast. "Tell me how he fucked you."

And so she did.

Chapter 4

Ana went to work the following day, just like any other day. Except, this time there was something unnoticeably different about her. None of her colleagues took note of it—to them she was typical Ana. Only Dennis, who like yesterday, having watched her exit her car and turn around towards the front, knew what was different about her; he could practically smell it on her from behind his office window.

Sometime around ten, he summoned her to his office. She was looking hot and exotic in a denim skirt that came a few inches past her knees, a tank top with a jacket over it. Dennis was sitting on the edge of his desk admiring her in her outfit. Ana looked like a butterfly coming alive in summer, there was a glimmer in her eyes that was intoxicating to see

"Good morning, Sir," she said to him after she'd closed his door.

"A lovely morning to you, too, Ana. You're looking good today," Dennis said to her. "Thanks. You're not looking bad, yourself, Sir."

"I try my best, but you're the diamond in my office, right now. Come closer, let's take a good look at you."

She approached where he sat. He pulled her closer to him until her breasts were touching his chest. His hand slid down her skirt and slipped under it and didn't meet any obstruction.

"Where're your panties?" he asked her.

"My husband fucked me all through the night,

so I thought I'd do away with panties today."

"Did you show your husband what I bought you yesterday?"

She nodded. His hands went on groping her body. His voice took on a smooth baritone as he was growing harder just having her here in front of him.

"What did he think of it?"

"He told me to try it on for him. I did, and he fucked me for hours."

"Interesting. Did you mention who bought it for you?"

"I did," she said.

"What did he say? How did he take it?"

"He liked the idea of you fucking me." She said it without mincing her words. Open honesty was something she and Alek shared and never something they trifled with.

Dennis' hand grasped her ass cheek, felt its soft, buoyant weight in his hand and licked his lips. "I was thinking of a repeat performance today," he said.

"Really?"

He nodded. "Yes, really. First lunch, then we fuck. But first, why don't you be a good girl and return to your desk, lest someone starts talking. I'll wait for you during lunch break."

Dennis gave her ass another squeeze before letting her go. Ana held her skirt up for him as she headed towards his door, swishing her naked butt side to side for his amusement before dropping it as she exited his office.

The rest of the morning seemed to fly away fast and she was hard at work calculating figures in her

26

computer when several of her friends tapped her shoulder, telling her they were off to lunch and asking if she'd want to join them. Ana apologised and said she would 'next time'. She waited till the office was empty before picking up her phone and dialling her boss's extension. He picked it up by the second ring.

"Hello, Ana," he said.

"I'm ready for lunch now, Dennis," she cooed seductively into the mouthpiece. "Good girl. But first, come in here for a minute. I've got another present for you."

Ana dropped her phone, turned off her computer as she got up and returned to her boss' office. His secretary had left her desk for lunch as well. She rapped on his door, heard a voice inside tell her to come in, and she did. He was seated behind his desk with his jacket open. She came over to his side and stood before him expectantly.

"You said something about a gift?" She asked.

"I did, yes."

There was another shopping bag beside his chair. He picked it up and led her to his lounge area. They both sat down and he reached into the bag and took out a pair of smooth, black open-toe stiletto heels. Ana's eyes just about popped as he pulled them out of the bag like a magician pulling rabbits out of a hat.

"Would you mind taking off the ones you're wearing and put these on?" He asked her.

Ana did as he wanted. He told her to lie back on the sofa and took hold of her legs. He caressed her legs from her tops of her thighs, down to the soles of her feet. He placed her legs on his lap,

27

reached into his pocket and Ana almost laughed when she saw he had a bottle of red nail polish in his hand. He uncapped it and began painting her toenails, starting with her left leg. Ana giggled childishly while he went about his work with the care of a world-class painter. It felt ticklish… and downright erotic, too.

"I always love a woman's toes and feet," said Dennis as he went on with his work. "You've got a lovely pair. It'd be a shame not to decorate it."

She didn't say anything, not wanting to distract him from his work on her toes. He finished with her left foot then went to work painting the toes of her right. In no time he was done. He raised her right foot to his face and blew down on her toes for them to dry faster before repeating the same action to her left.

"From now on, I want you wearing open-toe shoes. Also put red nail polish on your toes. This is how I want to see your feet at all times from now on."

She told him she would do so. He promised to buy her another two pairs of open-toe shoes to compliment the ones she now had. She put her old shoes in the shopping bag and went and left it by her cubicle before returning to join him to head out to lunch.

They went out to another upper-class restaurant and ate a most delectable meal; their feet played footsie with each other under the table all the while. They made idle chatter as they sipped their wine. Dennis enquired more about her husband's reaction to yesterday's events but merely skirted the issue. He didn't want to spook her about it. Though Ana

28

wouldn't have minded. She made an excuse later, said she needed to make a phone call, though this time she didn't require going to the ladies' room. She went outside instead and called her husband's line.

"Hello, babe," answered Alek.

"Hi, darling. I'm having lunch with my boss again. We'll be leaving soon to his place where he's going to fuck me good."

From the other end of the line she perceived her husband sucking in his breath. "Looks like you're out having fun and not working any more. I ought to give you a spanking when you get home."

She giggled. "I know you would, darling. Did I tell you I came to work without any panties or bra? I told Dennis and he fondled my ass in his office."

"Damn! You're such a slut, Ana. Did he let you suck his cock?"

"No, he didn't. But I'm going to, and I promise I'll take some snapshots to show you when I get home."

"Are you going to let him fuck your ass?"

She thought about it for a moment, then: "I don't know. If he screws my pussy good, I just might give it to him."

"Aw... I thought that was my territory," her husband moaned.

"Not any more, darling. I've got to go; I'll talk to you later. Love you."

She ended the call just as Dennis was stepping out of the restaurant.

"Were you calling him to let him know you were with me?" He asked as they walked towards his car.

"Yes. He likes me keeping him abreast of things. It moves him that way."

"I'll bet it moves you too, that he's moved, right?" He asked as he held her side door open for her.

"He loves it when I'm out having fun, and he likes knowing that I am," She said as she slid into the car and he closed the door for her then came round to his side and jumped in. Seconds later they were off to his pad.

Chapter 5

Alek was a graphics designer for an enterprising software company with smaller branches scattered across Europe. At the moment he was in the large office space he shared with other designers like himself, reviewing a set of algorithmic schematics on his computer and sipping coffee, when his BlackBerry phone muttered a '*Beep-Beep!*' sound, flashing light coming off it: He'd just received a text message.

He dropped his coffee and picked up his phone and smiled when he saw the message was from Ana. He opened it and immediately felt of rush of blood flood into his head.

I'm @ boss's pad.
So horny right now!

Damn! She's about to get fucked!
His cock gave a perceptive kick inside his jeans. He knew she was going to text him again soon, all he could do was wait. He dropped his phone back on the desk and returned to his work... except his eyes kept glancing at the phone, willing for it to make its '*Beep-Beep!*' noise again.

The sound came some minutes later and didn't waste time in reading it.

He's playing with my feet.
Says they're lovely!

Alex rubbed his chin as if wiping off a stain

that wasn't really there. His prick kicked up another nudge in his jeans. There were times when Ana knew how to twist the knife into him when she so desired teasing him to the ninth degree. This was one of those moments. He felt the urge to call her, to know what else they were up to right now. Was her boss kissing her? Was he helping her take off her clothes and feeling all over her body? He shut his eyes and tried imagining it happen. The picture looked sensuous to him... imagining her boss' hands grasp her tits... groping her ass cheeks... finger-fucking her till she squealed for mercy... I love this paragraph, you describe very well what Alek is feeling.

Another 'Beep-Beep!' sounded. He read the message.

Have tasted his cock - so very good.
He's going to get butt plug to fuck my ass!
Don't wait up for me, darling.

Oh shit! She was going to let him do it! Damn!
Alex threw his arms in the air and made a whooping sound that got several of his colleagues' heads turned towards him, puzzled. He apologised, said he'd just remembered something, then got up and left the room. Some of his friends' eyes followed him as he went towards the direction of the rest rooms.

Alex pushed the door to the men's' room open and rushed inside to one of the empty stalls. He unbuttoned his jeans and with a hand to his mouth to stifle his groans, he stroked his cock in rhythm to the projected image in his mind of his wife getting used by her boss. He ejaculated into the toilet bowl with succeeding grunts then rested his back against the stall's door, satisfied and weak. I like that you have him cover his mouth to stifle his moans – that's hot, shows how much he's affected by it.

***

Ana returned home in the evening a little past 6:30 P.M. She unlocked their apartment door and found the living room dark. She was reaching for the light switch when her husband's voice stopped her.

"Don't turn on the light!" He ordered. A table lamp came on beside the couch where Alek sat. He was naked and he had one hand stroking his cock with gentle love. "Take off your clothes. Slowly."

Ana didn't say anything. She threw her handbag with the shopping bag containing her old shoes on the sofa and pulled her feet out of the new ones she had on. She unbuttoned her blouse, swaying her body from side to side like one giving a slow erotic dance. She turned around after she'd finished pushing her skirt down her legs and shook her ass at him. She looked over her shoulder, saw that he was getting further enticed by her teasing and laughed. Alek restrained himself heavily from jumping off the couch and coming at her. She was teasing him again as she usually did, and he wanted the moment to last.

"Get on your knees and crawl towards me, you cheating slut!" He growled while still stroking pre-cum juice out of his cock.

Ana slid down on all fours and crawled slowly towards him with slick, cat-like grace, never taking her eyes off him. She came and knelt before him.

"May I, darling?" She indicated at his cock. She ran her tongue across her upper lips.

"No, you may not!" He snapped at her. "How dare you allow your boss to fuck you in the ass without seeking my permission?"

"I'm sorry, darling." She rubbed his thighs. "He told me he was going to do it. I just couldn't resist."

"Yes, you could. You could have told him that part of your body belonged exclusively to me. Except you didn't. You didn't because you wanted him to fuck your ass, didn't you, bitch!"

"Darling... He went into his bedroom and came back with a butt plug. I tried fighting him but he was too strong. I swear, I tried struggling... but he over-powered me."

"He over-powered you, yet you didn't cry for help. He came at you and you let him put his hands on you. You sucked his cock and then told him where to stick it in, didn't you? And don't lie to me, 'cause that'll just get me more mad."

"Babe, I'm not lying. He's a strong black bastard—you should have been there to see him. He held me down, pressed me face down on his bed and fucked me from behind. I tried to push him off, but he was too strong for me. It's the honest truth."

"You're lying, bitch," he sneered. "If you'd put up a struggle, then you wouldn't have sent me that text."

"Darling, please..."

"That's enough! I don't want to hear anything else from you. You're going to get what's coming to you, right now."

He got up from the couch and pushed her forward so she was resting on it.

34

"Don't you dare move, bitch!"

He came and knelt behind her and slipped his tongue into her pussy. Ana reached both hands behind and spread her ass cheeks wide for him. She bit her lip but soon gave in to her moans. Alex licked his wife's pussy up and down, felt the sensuous heat and sweet smell escape from within her. When he felt he'd made her wet enough, he hunched over her and rubbed the tip of his cock against her pussy opening then gave it a thrust. They muttered simultaneous grunts and Ana raised her ass up for him, wanting him to fill her up quickly.

Alek leaned over her and nibbled on her earlobe as his cock slipped further into her pussy. "Yeah... stay there and take your punishment! This is what you want, isn't it, bitch!"

"Awww-Ohhh yes, babe. Give it to me!" Her eyes were half shut in ecstasy.

"Oh yeah! I'm going to give it to you! Fuck you good the same way your boss did!"

He thrust into her hard, making her move forward with the couch. He fucked her like he wanted to wound her, but Ana had long gotten used to his thrusts, even though it still excited her. She felt bad that she couldn't reach a hand to her pussy to rub her clit. She desperately wanted to cum for him.

"Tell me, bitch," he grunted into her ear. "tell me you sucked his black cock."

Her words gushed out in-between moans. "Uhhh... I did! I did suck his cock, and I loved it!"

"Did he cum inside you?"

"Yea... yes! Yes he did! Ohhh... Uhhhhh...

AND I LOVED IT!"

That drove Alek wild as Ana knew it would. He kept on banging his cock in and out his wife's pussy. He groaned from the way her pussy walls seemed to grasp his shaft. It was sharply exquisite and intoxicating.

A moment later just when he felt his hair trigger starting to pull back, he pulled out of her and licked two fingers before inserting them into his wife's anal orifice. Her body clenched involuntarily from this and she gave a surprised cry as he finger-fucked her anal hole before hunching over her once more, this time driving his cock inside her ass.

He gasped from the tightness, held onto her shoulders while he fucked her ass. In his mind's eye he imagined that this was how her boss had fucked her. His thick black cock slipping in and out of his hot wife's pussy and ass, looking as if he owned it.

Alex muttered a lengthy groan before retrieving his cock, gave a speedy jerk and groaned as he tossed spurt after spurt of semen over her ass globes.

A while later he helped her up and together they went into the bathroom.

Chapter 6

By now Ana desired more of her boss, just as he too did of her.

Two days later she was taking a break from her work, gossiping with several of her work colleagues in the lounge area downstairs, when a voice went off through the PA system saying she was wanted on the phone. Leaving her friends, she went upstairs back to her cubicle and saw her office light blinking off and on. It was her boss wanting her presence in his office right away. She picked up some files from her desk and went towards his office. She smiled and waved at his secretary who in turn told her to go inside. She knocked on his door before pushing it open.

Dennis was seated behind his desk talking to someone on the phone. The window curtains were closed, blocking sunlight from entering the room.

Ana locked the door then approached his desk. She dropped the files on the desk—she'd only brought them along so as not to attract any eyes towards her main intention—and came around to stand before him. She held her skirt up for him to see she wasn't wearing any panties at all. Everything was bare except for her tan lines with light blonde hair on her vulva; she turned around and displayed her ass for him as well. She looked down between his legs and saw the unmistakable outline of his prick pressing against the fabric of his pants. Dennis' ear was still glued to the phone, but his eyes were on her. He pointed a finger downward, indicating for her to fall to her knees.

Ana did so and came forward to pull down his zipper. Her hand reached inside the open cavity and she licked her lips as it retrieved his semi-hard prick. It throbbed to life in her hand like an electric cable, pre-cum pouring off its purple-coloured, mushroom-shaped head.

Dennis' hand came on her head and pulled her face down towards his prick. Ana lapped her tongue up and down his shaft, taking in its musky scent, before spreading her lips to take his cock into her mouth. By now, Dennis was hurrying through the end of his call; he paused for a moment to suck air through his lips before continuing with whomever he was conversing. Finally, it came to an end and he returned the phone to its cradle and brought his attention to what Ana was doing to him.

"You're such a cock-hungry slut, Ana," he muttered between gasps as she buried her face down towards his waist, taking nearly every inch of his manhood into her mouth. "Such a hungry slut, you are! I've got some good news for you."

She stopped to listen. "Yes?"

"I've got two friends of mine who'll be arriving in the city next-this Saturday, the day after tomorrow. I'd like to have you around so you could show them a good time. What do you think?"

"Are they black?"

"They are indeed. You got any problems with that?"

"I don't know," she kissed his prick before answering, "I'll have to talk with my husband about it. He's never left me alone with three people before. I know he'd very much love to be there."

"Would he be comfortable with that? If so, then

you might as well bring him along. I'd like to meet him."

"I'll call him and tell him just that," she said happily. "He's really going to love that!"

"No problem, dear. Now, how about you keep being my 'Agency Bitch' and suck that cock like only a bitch would?"

Ana continued on with pleasuring her boss, sucking his cock as hard as she could. Her head bobbed up and down, and with her free hand squeezed his balls in her hand. It went on like this for another couple of minutes until Dennis growled tightly through his lips as he felt his spurt of cum shoot out of his cock into her mouth. Ana kept on sucking him, swallowing all the semen he had to offer. Some of it dribbled down the side of her mouth, but still she sucked him dry, before wiping her chin with a finger and licking it off as well. She got up when she was done, having tucked his prick back into its former home, then straightened back her hair and blouse. Her nipples were pressing against her top; too bad they hadn't been touched yet.

"Drive over to my pad from here when you're done closing," he said to her. "I'm going to need your pussy for an hour or thereabouts before I send you home."

"My husband and I were planning on having an evening out. I'll have to call him to tell him about my delay."

"Go ahead and do just that. For now, you're dismissed."

Dennis resumed his work while Ana swished her ass towards his door, turned back the lock, and stepped out of the office.

She noticed something was wrong with the way the secretary was smiling at her. The secretary's name was Mona, and she winked at her and indicated for her to approach her desk. She was a matronly-looking woman in her late-thirties. Her hair was brown and made in a coif. She had a thick-set frame with wrinkles lining the sides of her lips and eyes. Looking at her up-close, one could mistake her to be in her fifties.

"Sorry to stop you dear," Mona pointed at a spot under her chin, "but you missed a spot, right there."

Ana, embarrassed, blushed right away as she wiped the spot of semen off her face. It was then she realised her second mistake—she'd left the pile of files she'd arrived with on her boss's desk. No doubt the secretary, too, had noticed that. But instead of mentioning it, she kept smiling at her as though delighted with whatever had just happened.

"You sucked his cock, didn't you?" She whispered at her. "Don't worry about it. He's had his fun with me from time to time."

"Really?" This was surprising news to Ana. Never did she think her boss was screwing anyone else in the office aside from her.

The secretary nodded. "Oh yeah. He's got a big cock, hasn't he?"

She smiled. "Yes, he does. And he knows how to use it."

Chapter 7

Later that evening:

"You like my cock, don't you, agency bitch!" Alek groaned as he screwed his wife from behind. He had her in the kitchen leaning over the kitchen counter. His pants were down between his ankles and his shirt lay open while his hands grasped her waistline as he kept hitting her hard with everything he had.

Ana held onto the kitchen counter, slamming her ass back at her husband's prick, loving the feel of his cock inside her, though she missed that of her boss even more. Her skirt was pushed up over her ass and her blouse was open with her breasts dangling over the kitchen sink.

"Ohhh yesss! Fuck me, boss!" She cried over her shoulder. "Fuck me with your hot cock!"

They were having role-playing fun: Alek was being her boss while she remained herself. It was past the hour of seven and she'd spent the last hour in her boss's apartment, having had another roaring bout of sex in his bed. She had earlier called her husband and though he hadn't been happy cancelling their evening out, she'd promised making it up to him when she returned home.

Alek pulled out of her and led her towards the bedroom. He kicked his pants off his feet and threw his shirt aside as he trundled behind her. Ana went and sat on the bed, facing her husband. Alex helped her out of her skirt, knelt before her open legs and licked her pussy. Ana jerked her hips towards his face, telling him where she wanted him to place his tongue. When he was done, she came on the bed, turned around and presented her ass to him, wiggling it from side to side.

"Boss, will you please fuck my ass now?" She moaned as she then inserted a finger into a gaping asshole.

"I most certainly will, lovely white bitch that you are!"

Alek climbed on the bed, and grasping the wife's ass cheeks aside, he squeezed the head of his cock through the aperture that was her anus. Almost immediately he gasped as her sphincter muscles grabbed hold of him, wanting to squeeze his load of cum. Ana was having as much fun she could. Her hand dove between her legs and rubbed her pussy and clit while the throb of her husband's cock filled her inside. She grabbed the sheets and fell forward on her face when a wave of climax imploded in her womb. Alek leaned forward over her, pulled her face to the side and kissed her frantically while his hips went on slamming down on her. By now, his moment was getting closer to a hair trigger.

"Where did your boss cum in you today?" He asked. His face contorted to stem the tide pressing against his prick.

"Uhhhh... he came... my mouth!" She muttered between cries. *"CUM IN MY MOUTH!"*

Alek pulled out of her just in time. He grabbed the head of his cock, and though he spilled some drops over Ana, she managed to turn around in time and took the head of his cock into her mouth before any more could be lost. Alek felt like exploding, and muttered an "Aahh... Ahhhh... Aaahhhh...!" cry as his load filled his wife's mouth.

An hour later after they'd showered and lay cuddling in bed, their hands feeling over each other, they resumed their earlier conversation when she'd returned home.

"I'm still mad at you for making me cancel our dinner arrangements for today," he said to her.

"Why? Didn't I make it up to you? I told you he really wants to meet with you."

"As long as you're happy with it, then I'm happy with it too. When did he say his friends will be arriving?"

"This Saturday," she said. "Two of them."

"With him involved, that's making it three. Did he tell you where?"

"His place. And it's going to be fun."

"Yes, I can hear the excitement in your voice already. I bet you can't wait for it to happen."

"I just can't, darling. I'm even happier knowing you're going to be there, now, too."

Chapter 8

Friday wasn't meant to be a busy day at the office, except that week it turned out to be one. Ana couldn't wait for the weeks to move into June when she would be eligible for a month's holiday all to herself. Alek, too, would be away from the office by then. He had talked about them travelling to Turkey and Ana couldn't wait for that to happen.

Friday came and went, and all the while she was busy at her cubicle, her eyes kept glancing at her office phone. Ana willed for it to ring, and for the number to be that of her boss, but it didn't happen. She was typing a lengthy memo and because her eyes couldn't stop darting to her phone, she made a lot of errors. Just before she was about to mail it, she glanced at her computer screen at what she'd written and cursed herself. She deleted it and started afresh. Her pussy was crying out to her. She was fighting to ignore its plea, but that didn't stop it from screaming plaintively in her mind's ear. Often there'd been times when she'd been taken aback by her horniness materialising out of nowhere. This was one of such days. She sure could have done with a stiff cock right now to quell her rising temperature. All she could picture was her boss's cock pounding her right now.

Ana took a break from her cubicle and went to the ladies room. She stepped into a toilet stall, locked the door, hurriedly pulled her pants down to her ankles, then sat on the toilet seat. She wasn't wearing any panties and to her realisation her wetness had imprinted a circular stain on her crotch.

She rested her back against the wall and proceeded to masturbate herself. She shut her eyes to the world around her, maintaining only the image of a stiff black prick slipping in and out of her cunt. How she wished it was happening for real right now.

She was on the throes of reaching climax when someone knocked on her toilet door. Ana nearly slipped and fell from the toilet seat when she heard the sound, and for a moment she didn't believe it was her stall door the knocking had come from. The knocking sound came once again. She looked at the toilet's door and could only make out a woman's feet and nothing more.

"Who's there?" Ana called out while getting to her feet and pulling up her pants. "This stall is taken."

The person's only answer was another knock on the door. Ana, frustrated and madly angry at being interrupted, flushed the toilet then undid the toilet's lock. She flung the door wide open, about to bark at her intruder but instantly held herself when she saw her boss's secretary standing there looking at her. There was a knowing look in her eyes; the same type of look she had looked at her with when she left Dennis' office yesterday.

The words hung in Ana's mouth—*What do you want?*—but before she could utter them, Mona pushed her back inside the stall, turned around and locked the door then faced her. She pushed Ana down to the toilet seat, looming over her.

"I can tell you've been naughty in here. I've already locked the main door so we can be alone for a while." She grabbed Ana by the crotch then gave her an acknowledging smile. "You see? You're so

45

wet already. I saw you coming in here and knew this was what you wanted."

She pulled Ana's pants down her thighs, licked her tongue over her palm then brought it to Ana's crotch. Ana gasped from the cold, wet touch but Mona didn't give her time to relax. She was in full control of the situation in the stall, coming to her side as she drove two of her fingers into Ana's glistening cunt. Ana pushed both hands against the stall's walls and kicked her legs out, gritting her teeth as her boss's secretary rummaged her fingers in and out of her pussy. Mona turned to look at her, smiled at the reaction she was getting; she, too, was breathing heavy with excitement.

"Yeah... Dennis has been talking a *lot* about you. He says you love his cock so much. I knew you were a slut the moment I laid eyes on you."

Her finger-fucking went on relentlessly. Ana groaned till her voice sounded more like a croak. Her hair fell over her face. Her eyes were shut and she thought she sighted a nebula of exploding stars happening before her eyes. She didn't know when it happened but before she knew it, the stars burst and she climaxed suddenly.

Mona's fingers made squishing sounds as she withdrew them from Ana's pussy. Still Ana felt taut; her lips drawn in an 'O' shape while she sat there half off the toilet seat, gasping like a long-distance runner. Mona brought her fingers to her lips and licked off Ana's cum.

"Mmmmm... delicious," she murmured. "Very tasty! Maybe next time you'll be the one to do me the favour."

"As long as Dennis is there to take care of us

when we're done," panted Ana.

"Oh sure, I wasn't going to leave him out." Mona helped her up to her feet and straightened her clothes for her. When Ana had finger-combed her hair back in place, Mona undid the toilet stall's lock. "We'd better be going, lest someone suspects we've been up to something in here. You go first, while I wash my hands."

There was no one waiting for them in the corridor as Ana came out of the ladies room. She went up the stairs and back to her cubicle; none of her colleagues around suspected anything. Minutes later she spied Mona walking briskly past her office. No one would ever suspect her of anything resembling foul play.

Chapter 9

It was Saturday evening. An early rain shower had fallen over the city during the afternoon and it was a good thing it had cleared off before the evening arrived. The streets were filled with people out to enjoy a good evening, as were Alek and his wife, Ana.

He drove while she gave him directions to her boss's home. She was wearing a purple evening dress cut at her chest which stopped few inches above her knee, with black stockings under black open-toed stilettos. The dress rode up her thigh and Alek had to force himself to keep his eyes on the road just not to look at her, lovely, as she was.

They arrived at Dennis's home just before dusk and slid into a parking space. He turned off the engine then looked at her.

"Are you ready, my love?" He asked.

"Yeah, I think so," she smiled. Her lips glimmered red from her lipstick. "Say something nice to me."

"You look beautiful, always," he said.

"Thanks," she replied.

They got out the car then entered the building. Up the elevator they rode till they got to the top floor. She held her husband's hand and led the way to her boss's apartment door. She knocked on it and it wasn't long before it inched open. Ana was surprised to see Mona staring back at her from behind the door before opening it wider. She was wearing a smart dress with half-circle cups for her cleavage. The dress had a smooth flow down to her feet and her hair was tied in a bun behind her head. She had on lovely make-up and was looking anything but her dowdy self as she usually did while at the office. The dress looked tight on her and her breasts looked like they wanted to pour out of her dress.

"Why, hi there, Ana." She pulled Ana towards her in an embrace. "For a minute there I was wondering if you'd be coming or not, but Dennis told me you would." She let Alek in then closed the door and turned to shake his hand. Ana had already told him about her so it was of little surprise to him.

Mona led the way into the apartment. TV noise was coming from the living room when they entered. Three men were seated there watching a soccer match. At the sound of Mona's entry, they turned their heads from the TV to view their arriving guests.

Dennis got up and approached Ana, grinning from ear to ear while his two friends stood as well. They were wearing black jackets and open shirts.

"And here's the lady of the evening we've been waiting for," Dennis said as he planted a kiss on Ana's cheeks. "I'm glad you made it," he said.

"I told you I would," she replied.

"And you did," he turned and shook Alek's hand, told him what a pleasure it was to finally meet with him. "Ana talks about you all the time," he said.

"And she of you," Alek responded. Both men saw the irony in this statement and laughed.

"I'll bet she did. Come on in, let me introduce you to the rest of the gang."

He introduced Alek and Ana to his two friends.

The first was Maurice, an engineering consultant who worked in London. The other was Ade, a pilot for Iberia Airlines. Both men smiled as they shook hands with them. Maurice stood at almost the same height as Dennis, although he had a slimmer frame. His head was long and shaped in the form of a dome, with wide eyes and thick lips. Ade was of average height and thick set. There was an air of authority about him, and Alek reckoned he was the sort of man whom a lot of women would be dying to flock to. That he was a pilot made that all the more obvious. He had a well-maintained afro which his friends joked could barely carry his pilot's cap whenever he flew.

Mona pulled Ana with her into the kitchen to help her with the drinks; it was a good place for both women to make chatter.

"Have you been here long?" Ana asked her the minute they entered the kitchen.

"Going on ten minutes now," answered Mona as she opened the door of the fridge and took out a bottle of scotch and another of rum. "For a minute I thought I was going to be the only one to handle them. Just glad you made it."

Ana took the ice tray from inside the freezer while Mona took out glasses from inside a cabinet drawer. They were talking and grinning at each other like long-ago college friends while they poured and mixed the drinks.

"Besides you and I, do you think he's fucking anyone else at the agency?"

Mona looked at her. "You mean Dennis? No, I don't think so."

"How come all the time he brought me here I

never knew about you?"

"That's probably because I knew when you'd be here with him. I usually drop by in the evenings."

From the living room came the sound of music playing, intermingled with laughter. The boys were really having a swell time with each other. Done with the drinks, Mona placed them on a tray and together she and Ana returned to the living room.

"Drinks, everyone!" Mona announced as she entered the living room.

The guys got up and each picked up a glass. It was Dennis who gave the toast.

"Here's to a fun evening!" He said. Everybody clinked their glasses then took a sip from it. And just like that, the festivities for the evening began.

Chapter 10

Someone muted the sound of the TV, leaving the music coming from the stereo to play on. Alek took his glass and returned to his chair while Dennis pushed the centre table to a corner to make more space before coming back to join them. Mona was sandwiched between her boss and Maurice while Ade danced with Ana. Their bodies clashed and mingled against each other; bursts of laughter and giggles merged as one.

Alek's eyes moved from one woman to the other. Maurice was behind Mona and had his hands on her hips while she wrapped her arms around Dennis' neck, pulling his face towards hers. Ade was taking control of the situation: he had Ana in his arms and was kissing her while at the same time grinding his hips against hers. Alek drained the remainder of his glass then sat back to enjoy the show; his erection was throbbing within his pants.

Clothes began to loosen. Dennis and Maurice joined hands getting Mona out of her evening dress. Alek wasn't surprised to see that just like his wife, she too, wasn't wearing any panties, aside from her black nylon stockings and garter belt. Her tits fell like a pair of balloons. Both men reached for one and popped it into their mouth. She stood between them, resting her arms on their shoulders and surrendered herself to her delight as one of them massaged the growth of dark hair that was her pussy region. Ana was kneeling before Ade sucking his cock. Her hands were on his hips while he bent over her, pulling up her skirt to get sight of her ass. A

52

while later she stood up for him to help her out of her clothes. By this time Mona was sitting on the sofa with Dennis feeding her his cock from within his pants while Maurice had his head buried between her open legs. The moans coming from her mouth rose and fell sharply while her hips undulated themselves to the pleasure she was receiving from Maurice's probing tongue.

Ana grinned at her husband while Ade stood beside her, working himself quickly out of his clothes. When done, he kicked his shoes and clothes to the side then came after Ana. He roughly pulled down her dress then gobbled on her tits while his hands rummaged over her body. He was a predator and she was his prey, and the look of happiness on her face would have dispelled any from thinking she wasn't having fun. He lay on the carpet floor while she sat on his face, offering him her fanny while his cock stood in front of her like a tent pole. But not for long as her mouth found it and jammed it down her throat. Alek unzipped his pants and stroked his cock while he watched.

From the sofa, Maurice was now thrusting his cock into Mona, holding her legs on his shoulders, while Dennis took off his clothes. Mona cried out in response to Maurice's cock slamming into her. Dennis returned to them, now naked, and as if they'd planned it, Maurice got up and started undressing while Dennis took his place. He leaned over her and Mona's moans filled the room each time he buried his cock all the way inside her cunt. Her hands came to his shoulders and she held onto him while he kept on fucking her.

By this time Ana had turned over and sat

impaled on Ade's cock with her back towards him. She leaned back and moved her hips in rhythm to his cock slipping in and out of her. Alek saw her cum juice dripping down his shaft. Ade thrust his cock up and down, his testicles bouncing along, while Ana took him. After a little while she stopped and rotated herself, still impaled on his prick till she was facing him and proceeded to ride him hard and fast. Maurice came to join them. He finger-fucked Ana's anus while she was still riding his friend. Seconds later he indicated that he wanted a piece of her ass. Ade held Ana over him, her ass sticking up the air, as Maurice came over her. Holding his cock in his hand like a searchlight, its head found Ana's opening and she grabbed hold of his thigh and cried out as he thrust his cock into her second hole. Ana's body went into involuntary spasms right away and she had a roaring orgasm as both men began fucking her in rotation. Both men kissed her lips and neckline while she moved her hips between them.

Dennis by now had Mona on her arms and knees on the carpet and was fucking her from behind.

"Yeah... Yeah, that's it, bitch!" He growled into her ear. "I want you to cum! Cum for me, bitch!"

Dennis was breathing down her neck and slipped his tongue into her ear. He had one hand rubbing her clit from beneath her legs while still fucking her from behind: It was too much for Mona. Her breathing was already laboured and she muttered a lengthy moan as her climax washed over her. She fell flat on the carpet with her hips still in the air, but still Dennis kept pounding her from behind. Her ass cheeks looked like twin mountain peaks, the way his rod disappeared in and out of her. She signalled a time-out and Dennis withdrew from her, his shaft wet with the stain of her cum juice. He kissed her face and muttered something to her before going over to join his friends.

Dennis knelt over Ade's face and offered his cock to Ana. "Better clean it off, Agency Bitch!" He ordered.

Ana opened her mouth and grunted as she took her boss's cock into her mouth, sucking the tip of his cock before taking in more of him. She was in the rapture—she was at the peak of sexual delight. At that moment she would have done anything just to get satisfied. Her face and hair was matted with sweat.

Mona sat up watching the three men screw Ana, getting her strength back. She, too, wanted some DP before the night was over. She turned to look at Alek and went over to him.

"May I?" She enquired as she knelt before him, taking his cock from his hand and stroking it for him. "You ought to have a woman doing this for you."

"Ana does it for me every night," he said.

"I'll bet she does. Too bad she's too busy right now to attend to you. But maybe I can help out with that." She lowered her head and began sucking his cock. She slid her mouth along his shaft then returned to swallow him again, making sweet, throaty sounds while she did. Alek sank into the immense warmth of her mouth; his eyes went from her to the performance his Ana was giving amongst the three men.

After a while Ana was on her knees with the three men before her, and she was taking turns sucking their cocks. She stroked two cocks at the same time while one of the brothers jammed her face against the other. They were practically punishing her mouth. Strings of saliva dribbled from her chin all the way down her tits.

"Damn!" moaned Ade. "You sure weren't lying about this bitch, Dennis. She sure loves sucking cock!"

Dennis roared with laughter. "I told you, didn't I? Why else do you think I call her 'Agency Bitch'?"

Maurice left them and approached Mona from behind. He pulled her up but had her continue sucking Alek while he went at her from behind. She had her mouth engulfed with cock and nearly gagged on it when Maurice began fucking her. He slapped her ass cheeks, snapped at her to shut the fuck up, while still pounding her hard. Alek couldn't tell who was moaning loudest—him or Mona. A moment later a wave of sensation rose deep from within his balls and he announced that he was about to cum. He held Mona's face to his cock; she was still moaning on and on from the onslaught she was getting from behind. His body tensed and he grunted as he pumped loads of cum into her mouth.

"Swallow that cum, bitch!" Maurice snapped at her from behind. As if to emphasize his intention, he gave her ass cheek another loud slap. "Go on, swallow it!"

Mona grunted with pain and excitement. Her mouth was still on Alek's prick and like that she took in his cum down her throat. Some dribbled down her chin and on Alek's pants but she licked every missed bit off him.

"Come on, guys," said Dennis, picking Ana up to her feet. "Let's take things into the bedroom. Alek, you can come join us later."

Ana blew her husband a kiss goodbye while her boss led her towards the bedroom with Ade following behind. Maurice was still fucking Mona from behind and suddenly he pulled out of her and made her kneel before him. He jerked his cock inches from her face; every muscle on his arm stood out and he cried out as spurts of cum shot like missiles and landed on her forehead. She took his cock into her mouth and sucked the remainder of what he had.

***

Alek was still seated there at the couch when the bedroom door came open an hour later. Dennis and his friends walked out, all three of them laughing and elbowing each other with humour.

"Hey there, Alek," Dennis cocked a thumb over his shoulder at his bedroom. "Ana wants you to join her."

The three of them came and sat on the sofa to watch TV while Alek went towards the bedroom, undoing the buttons of his shirt while he did.

Ana lay on the bed beside Mona, with her legs spread lazily before her. Her body bore stains of cum and sweat. The room reeked of semen and pussy juice; the bed sheets were scattered and there was cum all over it. Ana smiled at him as he approached the bed. His hands shook with excitement as he struggled to free his legs from his pants.

"You've been a very naughty girl, Ana," he said to her. "And you're going to pay for it."

"Oh, darling, I've been so naughty," she murmured with a dreamy voice. She held her legs open for him. "Please come here and punish me."

And he did.

Chapter 11

The logs of wood were still burning in the fireplace. Bach had given way to Chopin on the stereo system. Ana was sucking her husband's cock frantically now, tugging at his testicles, willing him to cum.

"Such a lovely story," Alek muttered. His hand caressed his wife's hair as she kept on sucking him. "I love it whenever you tell it."

"I'll bet you do," she paused in her sucking. "Did I tell you Dennis will be taking his vacation in June, as well?"

"Really?"

She nodded. "His was supposed to be in September, but he says he wants to travel to Turkey with us. He's got more adventures lined up for us."

"You've already agreed to him travelling with us?"

"Yes. And I know you'd like it too." She went back to sucking his cock.

"Ohhhh... such a nasty wife you are!" He cried out seconds before he unleashed a torrent of cum inside her mouth.

Minutes later, after she'd cleaned him off, husband and wife cuddled on the divan bed, while the sonorous music of Chopin draped over them like a curtain of love.

The End

CPSIA information can be obtained
at www.ICGtesting.com
Printed in the USA
LVHW030146191120
672132LV00003B/54